皮皮與波西

For Enzo
A.S.

♥IREAD

皮皮與波西：下雪天

繪　　　圖	阿克賽爾‧薛弗勒
譯　　　者	酪梨壽司
發 行 人	劉振強
出 版 者	三民書局股份有限公司
地　　　址	臺北市復興北路 386 號 (復北門市) 臺北市重慶南路一段 61 號 (重南門市)
電　　　話	(02)25006600
網　　　址	三民網路書店 https://www.sanmin.com.tw
出版日期	初版一刷 2019 年 1 月 初版三刷 2022 年 4 月
書籍編號	S858150
Ｉ Ｓ Ｂ Ｎ	978-957-14-6543-2

Originally published in the English language as PIP AND POSY:
THE SNOWY DAY
Text Copyright © Nosy Crow Ltd 2012
Illustration Copyright © Axel Scheffler 2012
Copyright licensed by Nosy Crow Ltd.
Chinese translation right © 2016 San Min Book Co., Ltd.

小山丘官網

皮皮與波西

下雪天

阿克賽爾·薛弗勒／圖　　酪梨壽司／譯

小山丘

下大雪了！
皮皮和波西想出門玩。

他ㄊㄚ們ㄇㄣ穿ㄔㄨㄢ上ㄕㄤ
溫ㄨㄣ暖ㄋㄨㄢ的ㄉㄜ毛ㄇㄠ衣ㄧ……

條ㄊㄧㄠ紋ㄨㄣ的ㄉㄜ襪ㄨㄚ子ㄗ……

蓬ㄆㄥ蓬ㄆㄥ的ㄉㄜ外ㄨㄞ套ㄊㄠ……

……防水的靴子，
再戴上舒服的
圍巾和羊毛手套。

然後他們就出門玩雪了。

一一路上，他們留下大大的腳印。

他們用舌頭接住從天而降的雪花。

他們甚至變出有雙大翅膀的雪天使。
真是太好玩了。

接著，他們把雪橇拉到小山丘上……

然後從另一邊飛快的衝下來。大喊：

「唷呼！」

接著波西想到一個好點子。
她說:「我們來堆一隻雪鼠吧!」

「但我想要一隻雪兔!」皮皮說。

「雪鼠啦！」波西說。

「雪兔啦！」皮皮說。

波西好生氣，
氣得抓起雪鼠的頭丟向皮皮。

喔ㄛ，天ㄊㄢ啊ㄚ！

皮皮也好生氣，用力推了波西一把，
害她跌在雪地裡。

喔ㄛ，天ㄊㄧㄢ啊ㄚ！

皮皮和波西都覺得好冷好傷心。

可憐(ㄎㄜˇㄌㄧㄢˊ)的(ㄉㄜ˙)皮(ㄆㄧˊ)皮(ㄆㄧˊ)！可憐(ㄎㄜˇㄌㄧㄢˊ)的(ㄉㄜ˙)波(ㄅㄛ)西(ㄒㄧ)！

接著波西做了一件很貼心的事。

她說：「皮皮，對不起，
把你弄得全身都是雪。」

皮皮說：「對不起，我推了妳。」

他們決定一起回到舒服又溫暖的屋內。

他們脫下一身濕答答的衣物。

然後拿出黏土，捏了老鼠與兔子。

還有青蛙、小豬、小鳥、大象、乳牛和長頸鹿！

It was a very snowy day.
Pip and Posy wanted
to go out and play.

So they
put on their
woolly jumpers . . .

their stripy socks . . .

their puffy coats . . .

. . . and their waterproof boots,
their cosy scarves
and their woollen mittens.

Then they went out
into the snow.

Wherever they walked,
they left big footprints.

They caught snowflakes on
their tongues.

They even made snow angels
with big wings. It was such good fun.

Next, they pulled their sledge
up to the top of the hill . . .

. . . and zoomed down
the other side.

"WHEEE!"
they shouted.

Then Posy had an idea.
"Let's build a snowmouse!" she said.

"Snowmouse,"
said Posy.

"But I want a snowrabbit!" said Pip.

"SnowRABBIT," said Pip.

Posy was so cross with Pip that she threw
the snowmouse's head at him.

Oh dear!

Then Pip was so cross with Posy
that he pushed her very hard
and she fell into the snow.

Oh dear!

Now Pip and Posy
were **very** cold
and **very** sad indeed.

Poor Pip! Poor Posy!

Then Posy did a very kind thing.

"I am sorry for making you
all snowy, Pip," she said.

"And I am sorry for pushing you,"
said Pip.

They decided to go inside again,
where it was nice and warm.

And then they got out their playdough and made mice AND rabbits.

They took off all their wet things.

And frogs and pigs and birds, and elephants and cows and giraffes, as well!

Hooray!

繪者簡介

阿克賽爾・薛弗勒　Axel Scheffler

1957年出生於德國漢堡市，25歲時前往英國就讀巴斯藝術學院。他的插畫風格幽默又不失優雅，最著名的當屬《古飛樂》(Gruffalo)系列作品，不僅榮獲英國多項繪本大獎，譯作超過40種語言，還曾改編為動畫，深受全球觀眾喜愛，是世界知名的繪本作家。薛弗勒現居英國，持續創作中。

譯者簡介

酪梨壽司

當過記者、玩過行銷，在紐約和東京流浪多年後，終於返鄉定居的臺灣媽媽。出沒於臉書專頁「酪梨壽司」與個人部落格「酪梨壽司的日記」。